SEEING THROUGH

SEEING THROUGH THE SUN

Linda Hogan

The University of Massachusetts Press

Amherst

Library of Congress Cataloging in Publication Data

Hogan, Linda.
  Seeing through the sun.

  I. Title.
PS3558.O34726S4 1985   811'.54   84–28019
ISBN 0–87023–471–4
ISBN 0–87023–472–2 (pbk.)

Many of the poems in this collection have been previously published in the following journals and anthologies: *ACM* (Another Chicago Magazine): Seeing through the Sun, Folksong; *Beloit Poetry Journal*: Daughters Sleeping, Mississippi Trees; *The Clouds Threw This Light* (Anthology of Native American Poetry); *Denver Quarterly*: Fear of the Dark, Guarding a Child's Sleep, Cities behind Glass; *From the Center*: Through the Fog, Tiva's Tapestry; *Grasshopper*: Grasshoppers and Old Men, Heartland; *Greenfield Review*: Potatoes, Desert; *Helicon Nine*: Morning, The World in a Lake; *Massachusetts Review*: November; *1981 Anthology of Magazine Verse and Yearbook of American Poetry*; *People and Policy*: Tiva's Tapestry; *Point Riders Plains Anthology*; *Prairie Schooner*: Changing Weather, Friday Night, Bees in Transit; *The Remembered Earth: An Anthology of Contemporary Native American Literature*: Summer Again; *Sing Heavenly Muse*: Wall Songs; *Small Pond Magazine of Literature*: What's Living?; *Songs from Turtle's Back*; *Spawning the Medicine River*; *Sunbury 9*: In So Many Dark Rooms; *Trends* (Paisley, Scotland); *That's What She Said*; *Wind Row*: Eclipse II; *Wounds Beneath the Flesh*.

Ideas for lines 8–10 of "Folksong" came from an article by Thomas Transtromer. The term *Señora of Hysteria* in "Friday Night" was taken from a reading by Michael Brownstein. The last lines of "Wall Songs" are indirectly inspired by an introduction Joy Harjo read.

for Tanya
for Sandra

CONTENTS

DAUGHTERS SLEEPING

WALL SONGS

SEEING THROUGH THE SUN

How dishonest the sun,
making ruined cities
look like dust.

In that country of light
there is no supper
though the sun's marketplace
reveals the legs inside young women's skirts,
burning round oranges,
wheat loaves,
and the men's uniforms with shining buttons.

We are polite in the sun
and we ask for nothing
because it has hit the walls with such force.

But when the sun falls
and we are all one color
and still in danger
we tell each other
how this child was broken open by a man,
this person left with only fingerprints.

Sometimes one of us
tries to stand up to the light.
Her skin burns red as a liar
in fear's heat.
So in the light we say only,
Never mind, I was just passing through
the universe. It's nothing.

But there are times we tell the truth;
Sun, we see through you
the flashing of rifles and scythes.

Let's stand up. The enemy
is ready for questions.
There is light coming in beneath the door.
Stop it with a rag.
There is light entering a keyhole.
Cover it with your hand
and speak, tell me everything.

In my left pocket a Chickasaw hand
rests on the bone of the pelvis.
In my right pocket
a white hand. Don't worry. It's mine
and not some thief's.
It belongs to a woman who sleeps in a twin bed
even though she falls in love too easily,
and walks along with hands
in her own empty pockets
even though she has put them in others
for love not money.

About the hands, I'd like to say
I am a tree, grafted branches
bearing two kinds of fruit,
apricots maybe and pit cherries.
It's not that way. The truth is
we are crowded together
and knock against each other at night.
We want amnesty.

Linda, girl, I keep telling you
this is nonsense
about who loved who
and who killed who.

Here I am, taped together
like some old Civilian Conservation Corps
passed by from the Great Depression
and my pockets are empty.
It's just as well since they are masks
for the soul, and since coins and keys
both have the sharp teeth of property.

Girl, I say,
it is dangerous to be a woman of two countries.
You've got your hands in the dark
of two empty pockets. Even though
you walk and whistle like you aren't afraid
you know which pocket the enemy lives in
and you remember how to fight
so you better keep right on walking.
And you remember who killed who.
For this you want amnesty,
and there's that knocking on the door
in the middle of the night.

Relax, there are other things to think about.
Shoes for instance.
Now those are the true masks of the soul.
The left shoe
and the right one with its white foot.

The porcupine walked
last night's double vision of car lights.
Everything disappeared.
One spine after another,
light went out the brittle needles.

Today we drive past,
a man and a woman
talking ourselves backward in time.
Words go out
sharp tongues that have touched one another
rattling an entire life
of salty love
and anger that is its own undoing.

Porcupine, sleepwalker,
that defense quaking the air
breaks down.
In its eyes
we are on the other side of life,
still living.

Behind us the red-winged blackbird
keeps vigil on a cattail.
He opens his wounds,
a sleeve of fire.

I take it in
my own eyes to the river.
Everything reverses.
In the rearview mirror
the blackbird grows smaller,
becomes a speck of singing dust.
The road lumbers and clatters
beneath the porcupine's red and black
diminishing world of salt.

One way or another
the earth is after us.
Let's lie down together
before it stops us in our tracks.
Let's lie down on the bank of the river
and listen to water's pulse.

Latvian, a language without a country. ASTRID IVASK

The men are in assembly.
They speak, yes or no
and change the living
to the dead. Such is the power of words.
Even the hungry take to politics
and now we have wild garlic to eat
and hearts the size of fists.

This poem is written in the language
the presidents speak.
That is another reason to learn a new tongue.

Hear the sweet songs of sparrows?
Those are blood feuds
but the birds are safe if they keep moving
in neutral sky.

Our own songs are sweet,
me with my trail songs,
you with your *dainas.* *
Beneath our voices are war songs
though we sound harmless,
our fists disguised as hearts
because the men are assembled
with their yeas and nays.

Once, in the center of the forest
there was a pine tree
where all the spirits lived.
When it was cut down, the spirits
went to mingle like strangers
among the people.
Sometimes they look like winter sparrows
disowned by the south
with no place to go.
Sometimes they look like you and me,
their collars up,
pretending the wind sings trail songs

and *dainas,*
but even with mascara on their lashes
or sipping coffee on the way to work,
they remember long ago.

dainas: Latvian folksongs

Some memory, underground pulse
has drawn me
to these oaks and locusts
carved now with the initials of lovers,
small crosses and dates.

Those letters are windows of pitch,
a language of years
I see inside.

In this land
dead bark
is undermined by worms
as my own flesh
breaks down,
small designs working their way beneath it,
those arrangements of cells
which brought me walking.

A thousand figures
unfold their heritage of silence,
strange alphabet
sending out this message
into a new life
into words.

And listen.
The crows are still
talking about it.
Red rocks underground
are breaking open.

There are few moments of silence
but it comes
through little pores in the skin.
Between traffic and voices
it comes
and I begin to understand those city poems,
small prayers
where we place our palms together
and feel the heart
beating in a handful of nothing.

City poems
about yellow hard hats
and brotherly beggars.
Wasn't Lazarus one of these?
And now Saint Pigeon of the Railroad Tracks
paces across a child's small handprint,
human acids etching themselves into metal.

We are all the least of these,
beggars, almsmen,
listening hard to the underground language
of the wrist.
Through the old leather of our feet
city earth with fossils and roots
breathes the heart of soil upward,
the voice of our gods beneath concrete.

From beneath a stone
the black ants hurry,
the old dark ones
fierce as slaves
protecting new white larvae
from danger or sun.

Let us care for those who protect.
They are blessed with numbered days
and labor.

As for the young in their cells,
they are surrounded by white swaddling,
by what they must swallow
and eat their way through.
Already they push at walls
like our own children
covered in so many words
there is nothing left for them to know.

I did not mean to disturb plain life
or sit this long
beside the stone's country. It is late
and the men have arrived home
with lunch pails rattling,
and the women have removed
laundry blowing from the lines.

I didn't mean to find myself
wrapped around the little finger of this town
I wear like a white lie.
I didn't mean to find myself
wrapped around the doubting finger
of these towns.

The women are walking to town
beneath black umbrellas
and the roofs are leaking.
Oh, let them be,
let the buckled wood give way this once
and the mildew rot the plaster,
the way it happens with age
when a single thought of loneliness
is enough to bring collapse.

See, here they come,
the witches are downstairs
undermining the foundations.
The skeletal clothes hanger
has unwound from its life at last,
hidden in a dark coat
thrown over its shoulders.
Nothing is concealed,
not silver moths
falling out the empty sleeves
or the old cat with shining fur
covering his bony spine,
that string of knots
for keeping track of this mouse
and that.

Even the mice have their days of woe.
In the field and in the world
there are unknown sorrows.
Every day collapses
despite the women
walking to town with black umbrellas
holding up the sky.

What does he think about,
that man staring at the coffee cup,
rubbing out another cigarette.
He plants onions
that make me cry as I undo them.

Under his shirt the skin is white,
small clumps of shadow
that look like hair. He polishes his boots,
says we're going to move to the country,
keep chickens, have money.
But the kitchen gets painted
which means we'll stay.

Money,
I could taste it,
run my tongue along the rough edge of a coin,
salt off some banker's hands,
perfume from a woman,
that cold metal taste.

It's summer again
and June bugs fly through the torn screen.
Time to move to another place
where my purse with its dark
sweet smell of tobacco
is going to get fat with dollars
lined up back to back
rubbing each other
telling where they've been.

Between railroad cars
the sun slashes air.
Cattle in the field are set flying
through the shuffled picture cards of light.

Beside tracks, grass begins to waver.
A mirage, a hundred workers made of nothing
depart the platform,
sickles in hand, beating turf.
The grass lies down
in its own hidden life.

Something breaks loose, burning,
wadded papers with their news of the world,
a flammable rag,
the front-page story of a woman
who was rocking the silence
when some old love or hate beneath the heart
blazed her out of night's thin air.

Like the world around the train,
everything remained,
a candle flickered on the table,
four tight-fleshed tomatoes
ripened on the sill.

Even the skittish cattle
standing behind the vacant tracks
are at ease,
everything lovely and untouched.

The tree is all alone.
Its fruit is swollen with rain.
Yes, it is haggard,
the branches are bent down
and the leaves have gone dark.
The rain has added still another burden
and the red birds are too heavy in it.
They sing from the branches
and yes it is kneeling even more
and the birds are eating the black cherries.
When they leave,
the branches rise up after them.

So you came to surprise me
while I was watching the lonely tree
and red birds. So you are here
putting a thought in my mind.
Let's kneel down
through all the worlds of the body
like lovers. I know
I am a tree and full of life
and I know you, you
are the flying one and will leave.
But can't we swallow the sweetness
and can't you sing in my arms
and sleep in the human light
of the sun and moon I have been
drinking alone.
Later we will rise up
and shake the sleep from our arms
and find we were not broken down
at all.

Grasshoppers the colors of old suitcases
swallow apple leaves.
Morning comes in, a gold ship.
Like old men, the grasshoppers wake in fields,
wake the sound of rain
on the keels of leaves.
They hop freighters
and eat the cargo.
They sing psalms.
Every day is Sunday.
Grasshoppers, hay horses,
they wave with velvet gold and black wings,
disguised under looking old,
and we wave back
in farm dresses and nets of sunlight
on our hair.
Those wings could show us places
we never dreamed of.
But then, there are new apples to consider.
Hurry. Bandage the trees
with white gauze. It's a short life.
Save them before old men of winter
touch them dark.

There's something in the blood's stomach
speaking louder than hunger or reason.
It says, Let the politicians
live beneath their own decrees.
Let the talkers grow silent,
the prophets be proved wrong.

The wind is changing.
Lives fall apart.
It's a game called Shadow, Shadow,
and the rules explain the man outside
shooting at nothing
that holds him hostage.

This morning geese huddled in the prison yard.
By hundreds
they trespassed the barbed circles of wire
and guards on lookout in white suits.
The earth grew long necks
and spoke its own language.

There is something in the blood
and the geese have heard it.
Now they rise up
to journey through the labyrinth of night,
flying past antlers on barns,
flying over women's houses,
perfume maddening the air.

The sky opens
and a stronger world flies through, shadow,
shadow on the ground.
Let the talkers grow silent.
The prison yard is flying.

Dark trees built tall by the sun
uprooted by wind
we will warm ourselves against.
The morning air closes in
where trees have fallen,
light around everything
as the sun comes up
and yellow fire surrounds aspens
who held their thin ground.

Men divide wood.
In this season
I grow older
listening for the breaths of old men
to go out once too heavy
and I work harder
lifting old pine,
thinking how one quick wind
can knock large trees out of their earth
after sixty years
and how they fall
on the easy green arms of their young.

With our fire all will be forgiven.
The small words we said
and meant or didn't mean
are forgotten as we work.

With our fire the sun will burn again
like all these yellow mornings.
It goes on
blessing us
and now, just for now
there is the odor of apples and pine.
It is daylight
and clear
and I can see.

The pond is one of the world's hearts.
From time to time
some scaly fish of the past
beats up from the slime
like an old ache or love, then sinks again.

Crickets are pulsing in the wrist of night.
Sleep lays a hand on them and me
but forgets to count.

By morning, sit up! The pond is in
the clouds. Night in a robe of stars
did some alchemy, changed water
to nothing
and the old creatures are exposed
in hard air. What kind
of motel is this anyway?

Maybe it's Oklahoma
with rains of fish,
and the frogs, evicted for weeping,
falling out of Room 103,
their toes spread like stars.

Fog closes the world.
Glass is falling
from white branches of trees
hard
down air.
Trees lose distance,
move close,
lacing the window like frost
growing pale leaves.

The mountain is in my eyes.
White trees move closer.
Suddenly inside the eyes
a woman,
through fog she comes,
arms full of yellow flowers
for dying wool.
A bride's arms, gold,
cradled above a white candle.

And in my ears
her voice is weaving a whole life
into a sun and pale rug.
All her words,
the hiss of cooking,
the weaving hands
building a new room and window.
The window is woven
into cloth
and it sinks like this
into the eyes
and the weaving, the window,
smaller than the words.

Fog lifts.
White telephone lines outside
are carrying through air
all the voices
growing in ears.

FOR EPPIE ARCHULETA, 1979

The sun climbs down
the dried out ladders of corn.
Its red fire walks down the rows.
Dry corn sings, *Shh, Shh.*

The old sky woman has opened her cape
to show off the red inside
like burning hearts
holy people enter.

I will walk with her.
We are both burning.
We walk in the field of dry corn
where birds are busy gleaning.

The corn says, *Shh.*
I walk beside the pens holding animals.
The old woman sun rises,
red, on the backs of small pigs.

She rides the old sow
down on her knees in mud.
Her prayers do not save her.
Her many teats do not save her.

I won't think of the butcher walking away
with blood on his shoes,
red footprints of fire. In them
the sow walks away from her own death.

The sun rides the old sow
like an orange bird on its back.
God save the queen.
Her castle rises in the sky and crumbles.

She has horses the color of wine.
The little burgundy one
burns and watches while I walk.
The rusty calves watch with dark eyes.

The corn says, *Shh,*
and birds beat the red air
like a dusty rug. They sing
God save the queen.

My hair burns down my shoulders.
I walk. I will not think we are blood sacrifices.
No, I will not watch the ring-necked pheasant
running into the field of skeletal corn.

I will walk into the sun.
Her red mesas are burning
in the distance.
I will enter them. I will walk into that stone,

walk into the sun
away from night rising up the other side of earth.
There are sounds in the cornfield,
Shh. Shh.

FOR MERIDEL LESUEUR

Above gold dragons of rivers
the plane turns.
We are flying in gravity's teeth.
Below us the earth is broken
by red tributaries
flowing like melted steel,
splitting the continent apart
and fusing it
in the same touch.

It is easier to fall
than to move through the suspended air,
easier to reel toward the pull of earth
and let thoughts drown in the physical rivers of light.
And falling, our bodies reveal their inner fire,
red trees in the lungs,
liquids building themselves
light in the dark organs
the way gold-eyed frogs grow legs
in the shallows.

Dark amphibians
live in my skin.
I am their country.
They swim in the old quiet seas
of this woman.
Salamander and toad
waiting to emerge and fall again
from the radiant vault of myself,
this full and broken continent of living.

TERRITORY OF NIGHT

At sunset
the white horse has disappeared
over the edge of earth
like the sun running from the teeth of darkness.

Fleeing past men who clean weapons
in sudden light, women
breaking eggs in faith
that new ones will grow
radiant in feather cribs
the coyotes watch over.

All the innocent predators!
Even the moon can't stop to rest
in the tree's broken arm,
and at sunset the cows of the field turn away
from the world
wearing a death mask.

White horse.
White horse
I listen for you to return
like morning
from the open mouth of the underworld,
kicking in its teeth.
I listen for the sound of you
tamping fast earth, a testimony
of good luck nailed to hooves.

Even the moon can't stop to rest,
and the broken branch is innocent
of its own death
as it goes on breathing
what's in the air these days,
radiating soft new leaves,
telling a story about the other side of creation.

At night, alone,
the world is a river in me.
Sweet rain falls in the drought.
Leaves grow from lightning-struck trees.

I am across the world from daylight
and know the inside of everything
like the black corn dolls
unearthed in the south.

Near this river
the large female ears of corn listen and open.
Stalks rise up the layers of the world
the way it is said some people emerged
bathed in the black pollen of poppies.

In the darkness, I say,
my face is silent.
Like the corn dolls
my mouth has no more need to smile.

At midnight,
there is an eye in each of my palms.

I said, I have secret powers at night,
dark as the center of poppies,
rich as the rain.

But by morning I am filled up
with some stranger's lies
like those little corn dolls.
Unearthed after a hundred years
they have forgotten everything
in the husk of sunlight
and business
and all they can do is smile.

I like the smell of pine
in those rings
of the axe.

Feel the muscles
growing in my arms.

But the fire most always dies out
at three a.m.
cold nights
and I can't hold it
in my arms
alone.

Rich yellow blossoms
that tree
like a woman
alone at night
wearing perfume.

Not even the kiss of wind to move leaves,
not even a bird to touch the still arms
but far off in the distance
everything is a promise,
the traffic of birds,
the sound of the wind
saying, feel my breath,
feel my breath so close to you.

Señorita, he said, come dance with me,
come kiss me.
He wore a suede jacket.
I let him hold me in his arms.
Praiseworthy types often wear suede jackets.
I did, I held that man death in my arms,
Señor death and me out under the moon
dancing and the stars lighting up my face,
but his—all bones!

He put his cool hand
down my hip.
No, I said.

You can tell the bones nothing, si?
I know yours.
They want me
to see them naked.
He put his hand inside my dress.

I am a taxpayer,
I tell him,
you can't do that to me.

You've slept with the doomed, he said.
You come from those found
only by the buzzing of flies.
I know your cuentos. Go ahead,
bless yourself, but you are already puffy
around the eyes and your knees creak.
It's a wonder I still want you.
Will you have some guacamole?

I've seen the beds you visited, I said.
You don't make good corners
and you leave them a mess.

Will you have wild rice with butter and lime?
Just forget what I said about your knees.
Señorita, I will call you up
and don't think to give me the wrong number.
I always find the women whose souls live
in their fingernails.

Señorita, he said in his deepest voice,
I know the men you've been seeing.
They think with their genitals
and make love with their brains.

I stopped to think about that one
and held him a little tighter.

In North America
they have a saying
two things you can be sure of
death and taxes.

Death is more seductive
but still I laughed in his face,
no?

White cows in the lightning
left through a torn seam of the sky.
Mothers are at tables crying
but pay no mind.
This year I was suddenly old,
a mother,
and without a single cow to my name.

But I heard about the woman
who found an old hand in adobe
and how the doors of her house
opened all night,

so I know even my hand
has its own life
and my heart never believed
the end of anything,
not to mention the shank
which keeps getting ahead of me.

I won't weep at tables
at home or in cowboy bars.
I am done with weeping.
The bones of this body say, dance.
Dance the story of life.
Mothers, rise up from the tables.
Watch me, I will dance all our lives.
These bones don't lie,
just watch.

At the spring
we hear the great seas traveling
underground,
giving themselves up
with tongues of water
that sing the earth open.

They have journeyed through the graveyards
of our loved ones,
turning in their graves
to carry the stories of life to air.

Even the trees with their rings
have kept track
of the crimes that live within
and against us.

We remember it all.
We remember, though we are just skeletons
whose organs and flesh
hold us in.
We have stories
as old as the great seas
breaking through the chest,
flying out the mouth,
noisy tongues that once were silenced,
all the oceans we contain
coming to light.

The earth shows her face to the moon.
Murderers are exposed
in light's false astronomy of longing.
Lovers bare the silver oceans of themselves.

History, growing red in our shadow,
is written on that blood round pupil.

Take my hand.
You can see the moon rising
with our lives on it
and we are surrounded
by murder in the west
and rumors of war in the south.
The east's old history repeats itself
and there are reports of guns in the north.

Take my hand.
This river beside us is singing.
It is saying, *Yes*
to our touching of hands,
this uprising of arms
around one another,
the hearts beating on this hemisphere
and that.
Yes, the moonlight of ourselves.
What roaring along the river.
What fire, the moon traveling.
What singing.
And there are more rivers than this.

Sometimes I see a light in her kitchen
that almost touches mine,
and her shadow falls straight
through trees and peppermint
and lies down at my door
like it wants to come in.

Never mind that on Friday nights
she slumps out her own torn screen
and lies down crying on the stoop.
And don't ask about the reasons;
she pays her penalties for weeping.
Emergency Room:
Eighty dollars to knock a woman out.
And there are laughing red-faced neighbor men
who put down their hammers
to phone the county.
Her crying tries them all.
Don't ask for reasons
why they do not collapse
outside their own tight jawbones
or the rooms they build
a tooth and nail at a time.

Never mind she's Mexican
and I'm Indian
and we have both replaced the words
to the national anthem with our own.
Or that her house smells of fried tortillas
and mine of Itchko and sassafras.

Tonight she was weeping in the safety of moonlight
and red maples.
I took her a cup of peppermint tea,
and honey,
it was fine blue china
with marigolds growing inside the curves.
In the dark, under the praying mimosa
we sat smoking little caves of tobacco light,
me and the *Señora of Hysteria*, who said
Peppermint is every bit as good as the ambulance.
And I said, Yes. It is home grown.

The fevers of winter have flown away
and we rest in the empty palm of the house
like the shadows of animals
that lived here, chameleons
with starry fingers invisible on white walls,
deer breathing in the shadows.

We were almost
clenched in winter's fist
but the green leaves
are exploding from the trees.
Across the way, a woman's voice singing,
the song arriving like silk and spice
from Asia. Throw open the windows,
it's spring! All I held in
my winter breast turns back
into the world, an inverse body,
the universe turned inside out
singing and breaking through
the four red chambers of earth's heart.
Everything is alive.
The deer hooves clatter out of the shadows,
chameleons turn deep green.

I remember spring loves
and drunk kisses in the hills.
Things bloom in a woman's singing voice,
through open windows and longing.
Even nations are yielding
and there is the moonlight and her stars,
a flock of white cranes crossing the dark sky.

Do you hear
from the road
the horse breathing in
the solitude of empty space,
breathing out through men's initials,
the world branded on ragged sides.

I stop before the black horse
that has been owned and owned again.
Our bodies speak
across illegal borders
of woman and horse
while trains filled with diplomats
rush forward on metal tracks
that will never touch.

There is another language in the dark.
My hands touch the black alphabet of the horse.
The potatoes are alive in the cellar
and covered with eyes.
The dark chickens from South America
huddle near a warm bulb,
the heart of light
emerging from dwelling places
our animal bodies divine.

DAUGHTERS SLEEPING

A child sleeps,
ear to my chest, listening
while my own ear is turned
to the clear river.
She hears a remedy of lost sound
she believed was hers.

Yesterday white horses
scattered from her gentle presence,
their sides round
with new life kicking
and turning in the swaddling of flesh.

The river.
My heart is a window
like the one men working the dam
gaze into
watching, listening to the inside works,
the measure of some cog
turning water to light.

There is a beginning for all things,
a quickened pulse we listen for.
Even the dull rocks
contain another sparkling world,
the scaffold of light
building shadow
that calls out in an altered voice
asking the way a river asks
to carve faces of lost girls,
to unhinge a stone gate
horses pass through
like small clouds, luminous
in a sleeping dark landscape.

This is the earth,
skin stretched bare
like a woman who teaches her daughters to plant,
leaving the ants in their places,
the spiders in theirs.
She teaches them to turn the soil
one grain at a time.
They plant so carefully
seeds grow from their hands.

When they learn to weave
it is lace they make,
the white spines of a cactus,
backbone,
a lace containing the heat of sun
and night's bare moon.
The oldest child's sorrow song woven
so much like the wind.

This is the forest turned to sand
but it goes on.
Insects drink moisture
off their own bodies.
The shriveled winter cactus,
one drop of water
raises it from dry sand.
That is what I teach my daughters,
that we are women,
a hundred miles of green
wills itself out of our skin.
The red sky ends at our feet
and the earth begins at our heads.

Yesterday the younger one slept in my arms.
Today she curls beneath the orange umbrella
watching me. I watch the sky
for signs of bad weather
so my eyes don't swallow her,
don't take away the gold
that breathes her skin quiet,
the sun through orange cloth
lighting her like honey.

And the older one
sleeps like a stranger
to the country of fear,
but we move enough in step together
I walk those roads with her.

Beauties, I want to curve into your skin
while you sleep,
to suspend myself in you
and tell you it is a warm world.
Would I lie?
I'll say you are strong
like a people who lived so long
on fish, the glass scales
and white lace of bones piled up
and blew about their home
a warm snow.

It is impossible to close a door on dust
flying off the road.
So we sweep daily as women have done,
sweep earth between its two places,
air and home,
brushing even our steps away,
and the nightshift of childhood
we enter like dirty miners
whose heads give off light,
blasting gentle stones to let them through.

These hands of mine are working hands.
A twitch in the finger
sends out a mile of wire fence.
Alone all night, they remember other dark rooms
where children illuminated bones
with a light behind the hand.

I am not afraid of my skeleton.
It is a good souvenir of life
dancing inside an old shawl of flesh
dancing like straw brooms
nights in the kitchen.

It is yours I fear,
knowing it smiles when you send up
the white flag of sleep,
knowing the shape of your bony arm so well.
Daughter, the life is so tightly contained in you
I feel it leap out when our hands touch.
A single child
exploding like dust or mineral,
dancing, pale feet over air and home
not touching the sides of sleep.

After ten years
your head fills up with ghosts.
As you fall asleep
they rise
like the black hair
growing to leave your head.

In the distance
soft rain begins to roar.
Hail comes beating up
the imagination,
pale shapes grow out of night.

We climb a ladder of fear,
a backbone
to reach tiny figures
that fall through sky,
stars torn loose
and racing across earth.

On this rung
my face with its own fears,
too many to count,
leaps toward you and disappears.
Too many to count on these hands
that cover yours.

Child, even as you climb
one foot feels out the step beneath it.
Already it's in the light
reaching into morning's tattered fire of poppies
where the spider that walked through your sleep
drinks clear rain from a blade of grass,
its back to the sun.

Her body sweats in sleep
as if red fire entered her mouth
burning to speak,
exiling dreams
into the tense narrow bone of shoulder,
the black tangle of hair.

That life at night,
the life of a fisherman
sending hooks out
and reeling them in, empty.
Empty nets.

But she has not given in.
Even the taut muscles are working
to shape the woman's body.
The lace of nerves unravel
like a comet's tail.

Multitudes are suspended in her face,
the eyes of an unknown grandfather,
black eyes looking like turmoil
behind a closed door.

I would like to dream for her
a paradise of sudden flowers
breaking open a skein of light
but all the words I whisper
are people traveling
who lost their way
who lost their red horses
as if tethered to fire.

WHAT'S LIVING?

What's living-fission of mother and child?
Snake with tail in fangs? TAKAHASHI

The amphibious bedlam of mothers
opens a door and locks it at the same time.
I have come to bring my daughter fruit.
The first bite is sweet
as a shape formed out of dust,
as her dark hair I wash and comb.
The second is walking on fire
and the third,
that brine water cleaving apart
the way birds break off one way,
fish another.

Your sweet singing flesh
and myself, flaming ridge of back
edged sharp with anger and love,
this rare lizard who makes a wound
in the sleeping bird
then waits for the soft neck to weaken.
One hiss from my mouth
sets thin bones inside your ear
to violent motion, splinters the silent door.
We step so close to one another
we return to ourselves,
feathers and scales.

And the naked Medea
felt this love, wrapping her tail
about the beautiful ruins of children.
What's living?
The creature swallows herself
swallows all the bodies
struggling to death and birth.

White-haired woman of winter,
la Llorona
with the river's black
unraveling
drowned children from her hands.

At night frozen leaves
rustle the sound of her skirt.
Listen and wind comes spinning
her song from the burning eyes of animals
from the owl
whose eyes look straight ahead.
She comes dragging
the dark river
a ghost on fire
for children she held
under water.

Stars are embroidered on the dark.
Long shadows, long like rivers
I am sewing
shut the doors
filling the windows in with light.
This needle pierces a thousand kisses
and rage
the shape of a woman.
I light this house,
sprinkle salt on my sleeping child
so dreams won't fly her into the night.

These fingers have sewn a darkness
and flying away
on the white hair growing
on the awful tapestry of sky
just one of the mothers
among the downward circling stars.

FOR TIVA TRUJILLO, 1979

This is the month of warm days
and a spirit of ice
that breathes in the dark,
the month we dig potatoes
small as a child's fist.
Under soil, light skins
and lifeline to leaves and sun.

It is the way this daughter stands beside me
in close faith that I am warm
that makes me remember
so many years of the same work
preparing for quiet winter,
old women bent with children
in dusty fields.

All summer the potatoes have grown
in silence,
gentle,
moving stones away.
And my daughter has changed this way.
So many things to say to her
but our worlds are not the same.
I am the leaves, above ground in the sun
and she is small, dark,
clinging to buried roots,
holding tight to leaves.

In one day of digging the earth
there is communion
of things we remember
and forget.
We taste starch
turn to sugar in our mouths.

She lets go of my hand,
this child running after the red ball
she finds lost in the roots of a tree
and the tree reaching down air and space,
down where soil washed out
to earth's fiery center that moves
everything to life.

Red ball
the light is shining through.
The sun is shining
through its own returning to the hills.
It warms her face.
Through the circle of red fire
her hand is small,
dark fingers floating home again
unborn.

It is how we move,
this circle, this shape,
something we touch and lose.
Children listen
back the first heartbeat.

Last night I dreamed a vase,
red clay.
On it, animals were running,
their beating hearts,
a deer suspended along the rim.
Birds with sky in their wings.
Wolf. Bear.
Running a circle back to the heart of themselves.

This child,
the animals are in her
and will never leave.
The sky is in her face.
Standing this moment
she is still.
But in her eyes the reflections of birds are flying.
The sun is setting behind the mountain.

From the other hill,
evening voices.
Mothers call out the names of children
and we turn
and we go home.

Birds fly into the window and turn
on the warm rain
that stops
the shape of their feathers.

They fly to the window and turn.
For them the sky ends here.
For us it begins.
All the dry years
disappear
on the other side of air
where rain washes trees
and silver streamers frighten birds
from our hunger.

It washes down a nest of twigs,
soft feathers, woven sage,
and a blue thread from an old dress
that was mine.

My hand holds its own gatherings,
strands of a daughter's black hair, veins
blue at the surface of skin
so many years have fallen through.
Falling
the way rain we used to pray for
falls down the sky
swelling rivers into a confluence
that moves everything
to overflowing.

In my hand,
bones of the little people
who threw arrows and crows
from Spirit Mound
that grew like a woman
curving this flat body of land.

It's not our words
that absorb us,
not our stories of the little people.
It's the woman's body
preparing for birth,
the small heart growing
to beat inside skin
the world comes through.

We grow tired of words
and breaking down in them
the way leaves in the river
remember last year's sun.
There are other voices,
pheasant wings flying away,
fish jumping away from water.

We are on earth
and it is spinning.
The red horses, spirits or women,
are running.
Life grows in these fast rivers of blood.

FOR NORMA WILSON

Beneath each black duck
another swims,
shadow
joined to blood and flesh.

There's a world beneath this one.
The red-winged blackbird calls
its silent comrade down below.

The world rises
and descends
in the black eyes of a bird,
its crescent of fire
crossing lake and sky,
its breast turning up on water.

The sun burns behind dark mountains.

My daughter rises at water's edge.
Her face lies down on water
and the bird flies through her.
The world falls
into her skin
down to the world beneath,
the fiery leap of a fish
falling into itself.

And then it rises, the blackbird
above the world's geography of light and dark
and we are there, living
in that revealed sliver of red
living in the black
something of feathers,
daughters, all of us,
who would sleep as if reflected
alongside our mothers,
the mothers of angels and shadows,
the helix and spiral of centuries
twisting inside.
The radiant ones are burning
beneath this world.
They rise up
the quenching water.

WALL SONGS

Dusty light falls through windows
where entire families journey together, alone.
Mothers open the sills and shake the old world
from lace tablecloths.

Beneath flowered babushkas
immigrant women put their faith in city buses.
They take refuge behind glass,
lay their heads against windows.
Behind veined eyelids
they journey.

Brussels, perhaps, is their destination
where older women make lace,
wrapping linen around pins
and where the sun lies down in spider webs.

On the street
invisible panes of glass are strapped
to the sides of a truck.
The world shows through
filled with people, with red horses
making their departures between streets.
Inside that slow horse flesh
behind blinders
the dark animals are running,
shadow horses,
horses of light
running across American hills.

Everything is foreign here.
No one sees me.
No one sees this woman walking city streets.
No one sees the animals running inside my skin,
the deep forest of southern trees,
the dark grandmothers looking out through my eyes,
taking it in, traveling still.

Like a hundred white bedroom chests
being driven to the county dump,
clean drawers of honey
pass through autumn and stop
by the highway.
Noisy bees in transport
work their way through white sheets
draped over hives.

The air is filled with workers
on strike
and drones the truck deserted.
In its absence
cold leaves drop away from trees,
brush smoke rises,
and green Osage oranges are free
one moment before hitting earth
where dark women, murdered for oil
under the ground
still walk in numbers
through smoky dusk.

The air is full.
Bewildered bees are a lost constellation.
Through compound eyes
they see me again and again.
Multiplied
divided
in the confusion of a hundred earths
and rising moons.

Desertion's sorrow has not yet touched them
but it is growing death cold
and there is no place to go at dark
when the air fills up with sirens and suicides,
gray women wavering above the amber heat
of brushfires
and a thousand porchlights.

I would like to tell the noisy bees
there is a way back home.
I would like to tell them
there is nothing more than air between us all.

They lie down in the fields,
what labor,
born of nothing,
the geology of flowers
sifting together.
I hear them forming
as once I heard
invisible hooves of elk
rumbling over the land,
and heard the breastplate of Crazy Horse,
a man who listened to stones,
singing a museum back to life,
singing to breathless animals
the song of all people.

It was on his breast,
that song
that bone plate
that thin flesh
over lungs and heart, on skin
moving across the land,
the song of all people in a stone
he wore beneath his arm.

Beyond time,
beyond space
Nijinski heard that stone
and danced his body into the shape
of Guernica and war.
Who didn't know
gods live in stone and in our bodies,
that inside each other's skin
we hear voices
in the solar plexus
the heart
the ancient ones that burn inside us
rising up from nothing
in the dark fields of ourselves
like roses.

Beyond skin and stone and nations
all of earth's creations dance together
drawing together
the songs of warriors
drawing the dances
all over the globe
like a magnet
with her iron roses,
sand roses of America,
Indian roses,
the Russian dancing roses of flesh,
Africa,
the opening roses of the eye's pupil,
the singing mouth,
genital roses
heart roses pounding
breaking into the world
the tiny pieces of life coming together
where the mysteries in the ruins
of the dead
are speaking
in the red temples of the living.

When we enter the unknown
of our houses,
go inside the given up dark
and sheltering walls alone
and turn out the lamps
we fall bone to bone in bed.

Neighbors, the old woman who knows you
turns over in me
and I wake up
another country. There's no more
north and south.
Asleep, we pass through one another
like blowing snow,
all of us,
all.

Another morning walks in this canyon
to hold the town in red arms of fire.

It is morning.
The rooster is singing his daytime song
to the red trunks of trees.

It is morning.
A piece of all the killers is dead
and we are beginning to remember
how to live
in the pulsing arms of life.

Morning,
and I am here.
The sun is breaking through the window.
Come in.
Come in
and let the fiery armor drop away from us all
to the pure dance of life beneath.

Come in,
my arms and hands are empty
and we are together on this earth.

The black snakes are there.
Go in.
The white lizards are there
inflating their slender sides.
Pass them, one by one.
Even the red serpents with swelling throats.
Their yellow eyes will bless you.
Flying lizards with wings
and long human fingers
are leaving the ghosts of themselves.
They crawl out their own milky shadow
like sand coursing
one grain by one
through an hourglass.
The snakes will comfort you
with the two languages of their tongues.
They tell stories of wind blowing rushes
along branching rivers,
the feel of fine sand
on their singular sleeve of flesh.
All the living creatures have heard.
The snails glide forward on new silk roads.
Slender trees incline themselves.
City raccoons with poised hands listen.
The orangutan is full of copperheads,
each strand of fur,
and coral snakes
and they are burning.
The black snake and white
are one with the zebra.
The whirlwind arrives
from the night sky
and every crook in the road.
Stars are falling
down the armor of scales,
through claw white teeth,
through the clear venom,
the milk venom.

Stars like old earth
fall into black serpents
of the red soil,
falling through the hundred circular ribs.
The stars have listened
and they arrive.
Go in.
The leaves are flying about you,
and the fragile spines
are whispering, *Go in*.

The southern jungle is a green wall.
It grows over the roads
men have hacked away
that they may keep things separate
that they may pass through life
and not be lost in it.

There are other walls
to keep the rich and poor apart
and they rise up like teeth out of the land
snapping, Do Not Enter.
Do not climb the wire fences
or cross ledges embedded with green
and broken glass.

These walls have terrible songs
that will never stop singing
long after the walls have collapsed.

On one side of the wall there is danger.
On the other side
is danger.

There is a song
chanting from out of the past,
voices of my evicted grandmothers
walking a death song
a snow song
wrapped in trade cloth
out of Mississippi.

Open the cloth
and I fall out.

And the confines of this flesh
were created by my grandfather's song:
No Whites May Enter Here.

My own walls are smooth river stones.
They sing at night
with the beat of crickets.
They stand firm at 5 a.m.
when the talking world wants to invade
my skin
which is the real life
of love and sorrow.

My skin. Sometimes a lover
and I turn our flesh to bridges
and the air between us disappears
like in the jungle
where I am from.
Tropical vines grow together, lovers,
over roadways men have slashed,
surviving
the wounds of those lost inside
and the singing of machetes.

May all walls be like those of the jungle,
filled with animals
singing into the ears of night.
Let them be
made of the mysteries further in
in the heart, joined with the lives of all,
all bridges of flesh,
all singing,
all covering the wounded land
showing again, again
that boundaries are all lies.